DESIGN &

50 PRINCESS OUTFITS

Illustrated by Christine Sheldon
Text by Elizabeth Golding
Designed by Anton Poitier and Becca Wildman

About This Book

There are 50 princesses to dress in this book!
Each of them has a job or something they like to
do to give you a clue about what they might wear.
Use colored pencils or felt-tip pens to fill in the
missing parts with fabulous fashion. If you want
inspiration, there are lots of ideas at the end.

Have fun!

Add some little
extras, such as a
bunch of sparkles!

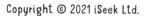

Copyright © 2021 iSeek Ltd.

ISBN: 978-1-64722-310-6

This book was conceived, created, and produced by iSeek Ltd.
an imprint of Insight Editions

www.insighteditions.com

Insight Editions
PO Box 3088 San Rafael, CA 94912

Printed in China

10 9 8 7 6 5 4 3 2 1

Let's go to the ball!

I like riding!

I love shoes!

Make me a fashion princess!

Pink is my favorite color!

I want to be a pirate princess!

I'm a poodle princess!

I'm a kitten princess!

I love handbags!

We're unicorn princesses!

I'm a mermaid princess!

I'm a fairy princess!

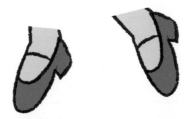

We bake cakes!

I need a tiara and stylish shoes!

I sing at princess parties!

I'm a princess bride!

I want to dress up as a princess!

I'm a princess hairstylist!

I'm a princess golfer!

Make me a princess soccer star!

I'm a princess granny!

We're princess jugglers!

I love to walk my puppies!

I'm a princess teddy bear!

Dress us up as a prince and princess!

I love flowers!

I need a pointy princess hat!

It's my princess birthday!

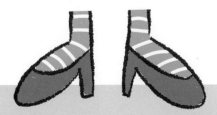

I'm a princess artist!

I like trampolines!

I'm a princess ballerina!

I'm a princess chef!

I'm going to a princess party!

Make us princess pop stars!

I'm a flower fairy princess!

I'm a flower fairy prince!

I like rainbows!

I like sunshine!

We like blowing bubbles!

I make princess jewelry!

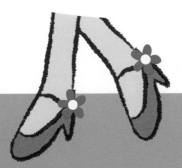

I'm a princess teacher!

We love to play with kittens!

I'm a super fabulous princess!

Helpful tips!

Let's go to the ball!

I like riding!

Stars look nice!

Red and pink go so well together!

Make me a fashion princess!

Pink is my favorite color!

I'd like to wear a fancy dress!

I'm a fairy princess!

We like to wear pretty dresses!

I need a tiara and stylish shoes!

I sing at princess parties!

A dress with polka dots might be fun!

I want to dress up as a princess!

Mix and match stripes with spots!

I'm a princess golfer!

I love to wear stripes on my dress!

I love to walk my puppies!

I'm a princess teddy bear!

We like to wear royal colors!

I'm a flower fairy princess!

My favorite colors are green and yellow!

I like rainbows!

I like sunshine!

We like bright colors with pretty patterns!

I make princess jewelry!

I'm a princess teacher!

1 2 3
4 5 6
7 8 9

I'd like to wear a red dress with a flower on it!

I'd like to wear a pink sparkly dress!